The Addendum

Books by Sandra Moran

Letters Never Sent

Nudge

As Revealed by Infinity
To Sarah Sheppard

Edited by Sandra Moran

Bedazzled Ink Publishing Company • Fairfield, California

978-1-939562-62-3 paperback
978-1-939562-63-0 ebook

Cover Design
by
TreeHouse Studio

BInk
a division of
Bedazzled Ink Publishing Company
Fairfield, California
http://www.bedazzledink.com

CONTENTS

Editor's Note

When I was approached to edit *The Addendum*, I was more than a little concerned about what I might be getting myself into. My reaction was much like that of Sarah Sheppard's. I was skeptical that what I was being asked to do was one big joke. But as I read *The Addendum* and then began the work of editing, I was struck by, not just the message(s) it contained, but also the questions it raised. For example, why are we just now learning of this new religious "truth"? What impact will knowing that we all worship the same force/energy/power/God have on humanity? And finally, with the revelation that these "nudges" have walked among us throughout time, will it change how we view and treat each other?

Regardless of whether *The Addendum* is accepted as the authentic word of a higher spiritual power, it *is* an interesting and thought-provoking document that ties in history, religion, and the commonality of the human experience as it pertains to spirituality. It illustrates, I believe, that there is so much that we still don't know or understand—and that that's okay.

While editing *The Addendum*, I had help from several people: Cheryl Pletcher, Shradha KC, Stacie Valle, Catherine Sherrill, Sue Fidler, and Ann Yamulla. I would also like to thank C.A. Casey and Claudia Wilde for their input in the final stages of editing.

I will close by simply noting that the work put into this document by Sarah Sheppard and the team of scholars was significant. It contains a great deal of information. My recommendation is to read it slowly, thoughtfully, and with an open mind. Right or wrong, if the message it contains makes us stop and consider what we believe and why, it has validated its existence.

Sandra Moran
Fall 2014

Introduction

If you're reading this, there's likely a reason. Maybe you're questioning your faith. Maybe you're curious to see what the Almighty has to say. Or maybe (and I realize this is the most likely reason) you want to see just how crazy I really am.

That's okay. As long as you're here and you're reading, the reasons why don't matter. Not really. What's important is that you read this *Addendum* and take some time to consider the message that it contains.

So, what, you may be asking yourself, *is The Addendum*?

It's a good question. And the answer is complicated. In short, *The Addendum* is the most recent message from the entity that many people call God but, in an effort to be inclusive of all religions, has chosen to go by the name of Infinity. This entity (or power, if you will) is the same supernatural force found in all belief systems. What's more, Infinity is the uppermost point of a mathematical trinity, which is comprised of Infinity, Innumerae, and Enumerae. Together, their purpose is to keep the universe (and everything in it) in balance.

Believe me, I know this sounds fantastical. I didn't accept it at first either. But it's actually no stranger than an omnipotent, bearded, white man in the heavens or a pantheon of Greek gods and goddesses who dole out favors or punishments as they see fit. When you take away the emotion from religion—any religion—and look at it objectively, none of them really make a lot of sense.

And that brings me to my next point. All belief systems must be taken as a matter of faith. Regardless of whether they make sense to anyone else, the most important thing is that *you* believe and that belief provides solace, comfort, and a reason to get up every day and do the right thing. One point Infinity constantly reinforced during our conversations was it doesn't matter what anyone else believes, what's important is what each individual believes and what makes them strive to be a better person.

When I was chosen for this task, one of my first questions was, "Why me?" Why, out of all the people in the world, was I, Sarah Sheppard, an avowed atheist and somewhat disenfranchised advertising executive, singled out to help compile and serve as the spokeswoman for the latest word of God? It turned out that it was precisely *because* I was a skeptic.

I'm not going to lie . . . I have struggled with this project. The information I've been given has challenged me—forced me to consider things that frankly scare me. But in the end, I have come to peace with my personal beliefs, though, because they are personal, I am exercising my right not to share them publicly. But, what I *will* say is my hope is that everyone who reads this has the same opportunity to consider and solidify what they do or don't believe.

Reading this *Addendum* takes work. It requires the ability to put aside one's own beliefs and consider concepts outside of standard doctrine. I know this firsthand because it was a constant struggle for me to keep an open mind as I conversed with Infinity and learned the truth about the formation, function, and tenets of Religion (capital R intentional.) It helped that these conversations were supplemented with scholarly research from a team of brilliant scholars and theologians.

What helped me the most as I went about this task was throwing out what I thought I knew. Though it may sound silly, I approached it as if I were an anthropologist who had been dropped into an alternate world. I started out by trying to understand the rules of this new place. I forced myself to suspend belief in what I thought I knew so as to consider the "other." Once I had established that framework, many more things began to make sense. And what, you may ask, was that framework? What were these "rules?"

- The Creator Deity (God, Allah, Mbombo, Esege Malan, Viracocha, Brahma, Pangu, Physical Cosmology) is the same force, regardless of the name ascribed to it.
- There is no one right or wrong belief system, nor is there any right or wrong way to worship.
- Humans have been endowed with free will and are allowed to make their own decisions. As such, the future isn't predetermined.
- All belief systems have been created to make sense of that which humans don't understand and to impose order on the chaos that is our world.
- Everything you think you know or believe is simply that—what you *think*. Your reality doesn't change anyone else's.
- Change is the one constant.

With that framework, it's now time to address the messages contained in *The Addendum*. What you're about to read is the story of Infinity, who has given us free will to make the experience of "life" whatever we choose. It's the story of a loving and compassionate entity that allows humanity to create and provide for ourselves, systems of belief (or not) in something greater than ourselves. And, perhaps most astoundingly, it is the story of Innumerae and Enumerae being sent to earth in human form on multiple occasions to nudge us into considering what we believe and why.

Regarding this last point, I will quote Infinity: "Throughout time, I have helped promote faith in a variety of ways. In the beginning, Innumerae was sent to earth in different manifestations—each of which were designed to inspire and to cause people to examine their own personal belief systems. Later, that role was assumed by Enumerae."

According to Infinity, we first see Innumerae in the human form of Gilgamesh, who ruled Uruk around 2700 BCE and who solidified some of the stories that later came to be detailed in the Hebrew Bible/Old Testament of the Christian Bible. Throughout early written history, we also see Innumerae in the human forms of the men we today recognize as Noah, Moses, and Abraham. We also see Innumerae appear in the fifth century BCE as Siddhartha Gautama, a human whose mission was to start the nontheistic belief system that is now called Buddhism.

In similar fashion, beginning in what we recognize as 4 BCE, Innumerae's counterbalance, Enumerae, assumes the task of manifesting in human form. We see him first as Jesus and later, as historical figures such as Muhammad, Joan of Arc, Martin Luther, Rebecca Nurse, Joseph Smith, and Mohandas Gandhi. In the pages to follow, the lives and missions of these more recent manifestations—manifestations that are much more varied than those of Innumerae—are detailed. What will emerge is an untold history that shows just how inextricably intertwined we all are. The stories in *The Addendum* detail the lives of each of these manifestations and the impact they had on humanity.

From the onset of this project, I was charged with the task of not only documenting the information, but doing it in a way that was approachable and in contemporary vernacular. For that reason, what follows is a summary, in my words, of the lessons and stories imparted to me by Infinity. With the exceptions of quotes from Infinity, the words are mine. Please don't think that just because there aren't a lot of "thou shalts" that this is not a serious text. It is. It's just presented in a way that is easily read by people today.

Finally, I want to be clear that my background is in advertising, not history or theology. To understand the historical, cultural, and religious significance of Enumerae's human manifestations, I worked with a marvelous team of scholars and theologians. To that end, I owe a huge debt of gratitude to Geoff Forrester, Abraham Schector, Salima Gregos, Fiona McAmis, Bart Harrigan, and Rainer Gunter. Their expertise in regard to religious belief and the individuals detailed in this document was invaluable.

And now, a word about what you're about to read. It is, and I quote Infinity, "a document for the masses." Each chapter is titled using the name of Enumerae's specific manifestation for that time. The chapters are arranged chronologically and include my narrative of what was imparted to me by Infinity, historical context provided by the scholars mentioned above, and direct quotations from Infinity.

As you read this, please keep in mind that it's a universal document that is not specific to any one belief system. If you're looking for overt validation of your own faith, you're not going to find it here. What you *will* find are stories of famous figures who, regardless of their belief systems, stand as testament to the ideals of living one's faith and making the world a better place. This is a new paradigm for understanding our world and the people around us. It's a new take on a message that is as old as time.

Sarah Sheppard
Fall 2014

CONTINUATIONS

Everyone in the world believes in something—even if that belief is that there is nothing outside of the here and now.

According to a 2010 Pew research study, 84 percent of the world's 6.9 billion people are affiliated with a religious group. Christians . . . Muslims . . . Hindus . . . Jews . . . Buddhists . . . Mormons. Those are the biggest, most organized religions. But they aren't the only ones. Throughout the world, there are people practicing any number of folk and/or traditional belief systems.

It's amazing, really, to have so many different ideas of life, death, and afterlife. But if there are so many, doesn't that suggest that one has to be right? And by definition, doesn't that mean, then, the rest have to be wrong? Actually, no, because at their core, all religions are just a variation on a theme. Don't believe it? Then take for example creation stories. The Jews tell in Genesis how Yahweh created the Earth. In India, Brahma the Creator formed the mind, then water, and finally Earth. The Hopi believe that Taiowa, the Creator, instigated "The Four Creations." And atheists believe in "The Big Bang."

The same could be said for the eventual demise of our species. Depending on one's beliefs, there are a series of events that foretell the "End of Days." Sometimes there are signs: tsunamis, earthquakes, plagues, and chaos. Sometimes there are messiahs . . . or incarnations on white horses . . . or second comings . . . or epic battles between good and evil. We see it in science, too, with the Big Freeze, the Big Rip, or the Big Crunch. Or there is the possibility that *Homo sapiens* evolve into a different species—perhaps *Homo perfectus*.

So, with all of these different shades of gray, which is right?

The answer, according to Infinity, is all of them. "Humans think I know what is going to happen, how it's going to happen, why it happens. But that's not the case. Humans have free will. They make their own decisions and create their own destinies. All I can do is let them make mistakes and learn—and occasionally, if need be, intervene by creating the *opportunity* to make course corrections. Whether they choose to take advantage of that opportunity or not is up to them."

Accepting the idea that humanity has a choice and that there is no "correct" way of doing things allows us the opportunity to change how we make decisions regarding everything from how we act to how/if we choose to worship. As scary as that freedom might be, it's also empowering.

To again quote Infinity, "I am the one ultimate force and am available to everyone in whatever form resonates for them. Since the beginning, my wish for humanity is that each person has a way of divining right and wrong and making sense of the chaos. Though every person, no matter what ethnicity, social status, or personal belief system, is endowed with free will, it must be clear that each action has a consequence."

When one stops to think about it like that,

suddenly, the human experience makes a lot more sense. We are, every one of us, part of a massive whole that includes not just the fact that we live in a global village, but also in the commonality of our experiences and of whatever overarching energy or force in which we choose to believe.

Infinity said, "I see and feel everything at the same time. All that happens in every moment is simultaneously my reality. I see the boy in Melbourne cry. I hear the woman in Bangkok laugh. I taste the flavors of the earth when the man in Antigua eats. I know the individual and collective dreams that come at night, and I hear the prayers of the faithful and those still searching."

We are, in no uncertain terms, part of the collective whole. But according to Infinity, we need to be aware of the extent to which that is true. In the past, the human population was such that there was room for people of common belief systems to practice in relative isolation. But that is no longer the case. As our numbers have increased and technology has allowed for travel and expansion into every corner of the planet, we are much more interconnected and interdependent.

"No longer can your differences separate you," Infinity said. "Rather, it is time for you to celebrate and embrace that which is common to all. That is the reason for this *Addendum,* and the message it contains. It is the *real* story—without artifice or condemnation. In some instances, it serves as a correction to previous religious texts. In other instances, it provides new revelations. In all instances it illustrates my love for *all* people and how, throughout time, I have sent Agents of

Change to guide and provide to humanity that which was needed. Each of these manifestations were catalysts—men and women in human form whose actions were designed to allow people to examine their faith, learn a life lesson, and appreciate belief in something, even if it is a concept that is greater than themselves.

"You are a unique and questioning species that is always seeking answers. This is good because the Earth is full of mysteries that have not yet even been realized. For every mystery solved, the door is opened for many more that cannot be explained—just as I cannot adequately be explained or defined. This is the magic and power of the human experience."

What is telling about Infinity's statement is that for every answer we think we know, there will be new questions that must be asked. Infinity noted in a very early conversation that it is The Trinity's hope that we never stop asking those questions—that we feel safe enough within our beliefs to look at the "what if."

As Infinity said, "Since the beginning, my wish is that each person has a belief to which they can turn in times of need or crisis—a means of making sense of the chaos. But just making sense isn't enough. Humanity must continue to grow and change—to ask questions that challenge what they think they know and believe. It is only when one embraces the unknown that true understanding occurs."

It's such a simple and yet difficult challenge. But it's one that, if we're willing to open our minds and explore our beliefs, is so worth the effort.

Book of Jesus

Just about everyone knows who Jesus is. If you're a Christian, he is the Son of God. If you're a Muslim, he is a prophet. If you're a Jew, he is nothing more than a man. If you're a non-religious scholar, he is a fascinating historical figure who traveled through the Middle East and possibly Egypt with a message of hope and kindness.

According to Infinity, much of what has been written about Jesus is untrue—just as much of what has been attributed to him (Immaculate Conception, being God here on Earth, divine healing, and miracles) is false as well.

In truth, Jesus was a man—a human man. That doesn't mean he didn't have a divine message; he did. It's just that the circumstances of how he came to be here on Earth and his role in guiding humanity is different than what is documented in the New Testament of the Bible.

"It must be remembered, above all else, that Jesus was born and died as a Jew," Infinity said. "His message was never one of a 'God' different than that of the Jews. His message was rather how people of the time should look at the Jewish God and what was godly behavior."

It was this message and the impact it had on people, like the biblical Paul, that eventually led to the early form of Christianity. Paul, more so than any of the other apostles, was responsible for taking the teachings of Jesus and interpreting them in a way that appealed to a broader audience. It's likely that Jesus, the man, would be surprised at the tenets of the religion that has been created in his name.

According to Infinity, there are two significant periods for each manifestation of Enumerae on earth. These are the periods prior to and after the Time of Awareness, an event in which Enumerae is made aware of the purpose of the mission and the angels (also born in human form) who have been sent to help. It should be noted that prior to the Time of Awareness, Enumerae is unaware of the fact that his or her life has a purpose other than that of every other human.

Jesus Before the Time of Awareness

The human manifestation of Enumerae as Jesus was born in March of what is today known as 4 BCE. Little is recorded in the existing religious texts about the years between his birth and his teaching, in large part because there weren't many people who could read and write and, more importantly, because there wasn't much to tell. Jesus was an ordinary child who, aside from having a capacity for recalling, understanding, and interpreting the oral Torah, was unremarkable.

Despite later claims that he was the product of Immaculate Conception, Jesus was the biological son of Joseph and Mary. Though it is true that he was conceived before they were married, the situation was soon rectified. In his youth, Jesus apprenticed to his father, played with his younger brothers and sisters, and when he was thirteen, had his bar mitzvah. Again, it should be noted that Jesus had no idea of his true mission at this time.

Little is also known about Jesus during his twenties. There are numerous theories as to what he did and why. The truth is less interesting than most of these stories. Because of his facility for learning and recitation, when Jesus was nineteen, he traveled to Egypt where he studied with the Theraputae and learned, among other skills, the art of healing and magic. He later journeyed to Palestine where he studied with the Essenes. It was the knowledge he gained in these two experiences, combined with Jesus's natural intellect, charisma, and showmanship, that later allowed him to perform "miracles" as he traveled throughout Galilee and Judea preaching a message of love, kindness, and forgiveness to the assembled Jews.

Jesus After the Time of Awareness

When Jesus turned thirty, he was made aware of his mission on earth by Infinity. This "awareness event" came at the hands of his cousin, John, who held him beneath the baptismal waters of the Jordan River to the point of drowning. It was during this separation from his consciousness that Jesus came to understand what was expected of him—that he was expected to travel the land with his message of how to be a more "godly" person. He also learned that along the way he would meet other energies/angels/entities in human form who would become disciples and help spread the message. The final part of his mission would be his death at the hands of the political leaders of the time, the Romans.

"It must be remembered," Infinity said, "that despite the circumstances that launched his ministry and the task with which he was charged, Jesus was a human with very real human emotions. And, because he was flesh and blood, he also was endowed with the gift of free will. It should come as no surprise, then, that when he fell in love with Mary Magdalene, he acted upon it."

The omission of this detail, according to Infinity, is one of many errors in the Christian New Testament—as is the reason for Jesus' crucifixion. According to the Bible, Jesus was executed for treason—for allegedly calling himself the King of the Jews. In a time where there could only be one ruler, this was perceived as a threat to the Roman Emperor, Tiberius. The Romans, represented by Pontius Pilate who was in Jerusalem to keep the peace during the Passover observance, in fact tried several times to free Jesus.

For the mission to be completed, though, that could not happen.

To quote Infinity, "Just as several of the disciples were angels, so too was Caiaphas, the president of the Sanhedrin. Despite being a Jewish religious leader, his role in this manifestation event was to ensure that Jesus was very publicly tried and executed in such a way that guaranteed that the message of kindness, forgiveness, and belief in a single Jewish God lived on. To accomplish this, he had no choice but to insist that Jesus's presence undermined the power of the establishment."

Though asphyxia would have impacted Jesus's

ability to speak, his request that the Romans be forgiven, "for they know not what they do," was telling. It was also part of the plan—as was the story, after his death, of the resurrection.

According to Infinity, just as Judas was responsible for "betraying" Jesus and Caiaphas was tasked with ordering his execution, Mary Magdalene, was responsible for telling the story of the resurrection as an illustration of the rewards that come from following the path of love and forgiveness in life. With the help of the other disciples, the physical body of Jesus was secretly removed from the tomb, and Mary began to share her "eye witness account" of the resurrection.

The Formation of Christianity

As noted previously, none of the activities detailed above were designed to create a new religious belief system. Rather, the hope was that the philosophy that Jesus embodied would live on in a more peaceful and benevolent society. Angels, in the human form of Peter and James, continued to spread Jesus's message. They orally shared their stories with whoever would listen.

At first, their following was small and they faced persecution at the hands of Jewish religious zealots who thought this new take on belief, which was coming to be called Christianity, was blasphemous. One of the most aggressive of these zealots was Saul—a human who had embarked on a personal quest to stamp out the teachings of Jesus by persecuting anyone who was propagating the message.

In an unexpected twist of irony, Saul suffered heat stroke while traveling from Jerusalem to Damascus to arrest people known to be Christians. His obsession with Christianity manifested in a vision of Jesus and in that instant, his entire perception of what he thought he believed changed. Rather than continuing to condemn Christians, Saul, who changed his name to Paul, despite never having met Jesus, became the spokesperson for the belief, traveling throughout present day Israel, Turkey, and Greece with his personal interpretation of Jesus's message.

As noted by Infinity, this is an example of how human free will is the engine that drives religion. Left to his own devices, Paul went on to change the tenets of what constituted Christianity. By relaxing the food taboos and removing the stipulation that gentiles (pagans) had to be circumcised, Paul was able to mold Christianity to what *he* believed was most appealing. To be a Christian, followers only had to have faith in Jesus's death and resurrection.

We know of his actions through his letters—letters that are later, along with anonymously authored recountings of the orally-transmitted stories of Jesus's death and resurrection, compiled into what is today known as the New Testament.

So with this new knowledge of how Christianity came to be, where does that leave us? What does it mean that a belief system that is practiced by 32 percent of the world's population is based on a message that was co-opted from one man's ministry and manipulated and marketed to enhance another man's power?

To cite Infinity, what this means is "a societal

and religious need was met." By being born as a human, living as an example of forgiveness and compassion, and later inspiring others such as Paul to take the message to a higher level, ultimately provided humanity what it desired.

"It is about providing people what they need," Infinity said. "There is no right or wrong; there simply *is*. The power of belief is the key. If one chooses to believe Paul's interpretation that Jesus was the Son of God, then he was. If one chooses to instead believe that Jesus was a prophet, then he was."

This interpretation . . . this lesson . . . is a powerful one. If we can distance ourselves from the emotion of being right and instead see the commonality and power of "belief," then suddenly the differences in (or the evolution of) a particular belief system ceases to matter. What becomes important is the role it assumes in our lives. And this, according to Infinity, was the lesson to be derived from the Book of Jesus.

Book of Muhammad

One of the most important aspects of the human experience—and one that can be seen time and again—is the importance of change.

"Nothing," Infinity said, "can stay the same forever or it will cease to be relevant and functional. Everything, even if it is an idea, must continue to grow and change."

It becomes clear that this is indeed true when applying these words to the world around us. We see it in evolution and in the concepts of adaptation and natural selection. The same applies for cultural constructs—the things people do to survive and advance. One only needs to look at the technology at our disposal to appreciate how advancements change how we do things.

The same applies to religion. Given the state of ongoing change around us, belief systems have to change and grow to meet the needs of the practitioners. In some instances, new faiths must be created. An early example of this is seen with the development of Islamic belief.

A clear division based on religious affiliation began as the concept of Christianity spread through Egypt, the Middle East, and Europe. This was complicated as Jews and Christians, not that far removed from a single belief, struggled to find their boundaries. There also existed a group of people whose needs were met by none of the existing religions.

And so, Infinity once again sent Enumerae to the Earth. But this time, it was not simply to bring about change. After seeing what Paul had accomplished with the formation of Christianity, Infinity charged Enumerae with the task of being born into the human form of a man named Muhammad—a man whose mission was to serve as a messenger, a prophet, and a salve to those who were struggling to find a way to believe in something larger than themselves.

"The needs of many were being met," Infinity said. "But not all. For some, the existing belief systems were not rigid enough. Or they were not inclusive of women or the indentured. It also became apparent that people were so concerned with the day-to-day tasks of living, they forgot to be mindful of the belief system that provided them what they needed. As Muhammad, Enumerae's mission was to provide a new religion in the form of Islamic belief and to serve as a religious catalyst—to make Christians more Christian and the Jews more Jewish."

Muhammad Before the Time of Awareness

According to Infinity, Enumerae was born into the human form of Muhammad in the year 570 CE, in the Arabian city of Mecca. As had been the case with Jesus, Enumerae was a rather unremarkable boy with the exception of what was a somewhat tragic childhood.

To quote Infinity, "The life lessons that Muhammad had to learn in preparation for his mission required that he endure hardship. He was orphaned and raised by his uncle so he could learn gratitude and the value of family. He worked as a shepherd so he could learn to tend to the needs of others. Despite being an introvert, he was made to be a merchant, managing the caravans on the northern leg of the journey to Syria so he could learn to interact with people of different faiths. All of this was necessary for the role he was about to assume."

Unlike in the previous manifestation, however, Enumerae, as Muhammad, was allowed to marry and father children. It was an unconventional marriage for its time because it was based on love and respect. As a result, Khadijah, who had been Mary Magdalene in the past and who would play a pivotal role in future manifestations, was Muhammad's staunchest supporter.

Muhammad After the Time of Awareness

According to Infinity, Muhammad came to understand his true identity and his mission at the age of forty in a cave on Mount Hira. Much as had been the case with Jesus, where the traumatic event of nearly drowning put him in a state of consciousness that revealed his true purpose, Muhammad, too, lost consciousness. The cause of his awareness, however, was at the hands of what we now call epilepsy.

"Muhammad had always struggled to fit in to Arab society," Infinity said. "His natural introversion and struggles with depression drove him to often retreat to Mount Hira where he would fast and meditate on issues such as social inequity and what he saw as rampant vice."

As a direct descendent of Ishmael and Abraham, Muhammad's faith was central to who he was and how he conducted himself. In his opinion, the Arab nation was not being true to the pure faith handed down by his ancestors. More to the point, he believed that Jews and Christians were worshiping false idols. Much of his prayer and meditation focused on these issues.

"Muhammad's Awareness Event came at the hands of the angel, Gabriel," Infinity said. "It was during one of his meditation retreats that he had his first epileptic seizure. And during this altered state of consciousness, he learned the true nature of his time on earth—to create and spread the news of the Islamic belief. This included the creation of a new text that would be called the Qur'an."

"One of the lessons we learned from Jesus, and the post-mortem creation of the New Testament, was that if we didn't craft and produce the message ourselves, it would be manipulated, co-opted, and undergo extensive editing. For the Qur'an to truly embody the teachings of this new belief, the document had to be dictated by Muhammad and written down without change. It was our first attempt at crafting an unalterable message."

Though the dictation of the Qur'an came later, the work to begin sharing the message of this new belief system began immediately. Shortly after Muhammad's Time of Awareness, Khadijah and the rest of the Angels sent to facilitate the mission became aware of their roles.

Muhammad's message was deceptively simple and appealed to the people who desired a more rigorous belief system. To live a righteous life, Muslims needed to reject idolatry and worship the one, true god, Allah; believe in the rewards of heaven and the punishment of hell; strive for a society with social and economic equity; and give voice to the lower classes, women, and slaves. In many regards, the message of compassion, equality, and value for humankind was not that dissimilar from that of Jesus.

Enumerae, as Muhammad, was charged with spreading this message throughout the Arab nation—which is what he did, despite being exiled from Mecca and enduring numerous assassination attempts by tribal and political leaders who feared a change in the status quo.

Muhammad changed the social, cultural, and religious dynamic of the region to the point that within fifty years of his death, the Islamic empire covered one-third of the Old World. We continue to see the result of Enumerae's manifestation as Muhammad in the fact that 1.6 billion (more than 23 percent of the world's population) identify as Muslim. And its relevance and resonance continues to be reflected in that it's one of the fastest growing religions throughout the world—this despite the fact that many of the tenets are markedly different from those of Christianity, Hinduism, Buddhism, and Judaism. Yet, there continues to be distrust of Muslims. Why?

The simple answer? Fear.

"Throughout time, every religion has been vilified by practitioners of others," Infinity said. "It is the fear of that which is different. But the question that you should ask yourself is, 'why, if you are secure in your faith, should you care about or fear what anyone else believes or does?' Throughout time I have provided, for all humans, belief systems that resonate for them. And, throughout time I have given humans the gift of free will to choose what is right for them. Why should this universal freedom be the basis for fear?"

It is a very good question. Why do we fear that which is different? And more to the point, why do we, as humans, try to subjugate others? Consider the age-old debate of nature versus nurture. Is who we are inherent or are we created in such a way that we are shaped by our environment? Is the hatred and fear of that which is different a learned behavior? If it is, that means that we have the ability to change.

Infinity has commissioned this *Addendum* to show the universality of the human experience. If we are to survive as a species, now, even more than ever before, we need to take from the lessons of Jesus and Muhammad and focus on forgiveness and tolerance.

Book of Joan of Arc

One of the points that Infinity repeatedly stressed in the creation of this *Addendum* is that although there is an oversight role on the part of the Trinity, the future, itself, is unscripted. Our gift of free will allows us to succeed or fail based on the decisions we make.

To allow those we love the ability to make their own mistakes is a difficult challenge, although it is possibly easier for Infinity than for humans. Think, for example, of the dilemma faced by parents as they watch their children grow and make mistakes as they experience the world. How hard is it to stand back and let them learn from their mistakes and only step in when they are in too deep?

It's not dissimilar to the role played by Infinity in humanity's maturation process.

"Humans have been endowed with the ability to make their own decisions and create their own destinies," Infinity said. "All I can do is let them make mistakes and learn. And occasionally, if need be, I can institute course corrections—though I try not to. Rather, I make available to humans what they need. Whether they choose to take it or not is up to them."

One such opportunity for a "course correction," and the subject of this next manifestation, is Joan of Arc.

To quote Infinity, "The more widespread a belief system becomes, the more complicated and interdependent variables outside of faith—variables such as politics, economics, and power—become. Such was the state of Christianity in the year 1412—the year of Joan's birth or, as she was known in France, Jeanne d'Arc."

Joan Before the Time of Awareness

According to Infinity, several of the manifestations of Enumerae have been sent at times where there is significant cultural or social change. This is especially true when Enumerae returned to earth as the human Joan of Arc, in the middle of the Hundred Years' War between France and England, who ruled over much of France at the time.

Although wars had been fought in the past that were of a similar scale, this particular conflict was significant because it was so long-standing and impactful on such a significant diversity of cultural groups. It was one of many early examples of the web of interconnectivity that is such an inescapable aspect of our lives today.

As explained by Infinity, "For this manifestation, I chose to have Enumerae born into the human form of a young, peasant girl who, for all intents and purposes, was considered by society as someone without power. Because the world was becoming a much more connected and divisive place, it was imperative to remind humanity of the ability of one person to exact change if they are steadfast in their beliefs. Additionally, people in Europe at the time needed to be reminded that belief in something higher than—something greater than—oneself was necessary if they were to survive."

As had been the case with previous manifestations, Enumerae, in the human form of Joan, was rather unextraordinary. Though she was more devout than most children her age, her only other distinguishing feature was that she, like Jesus and Muhammad before her, craved solitude. It was not uncommon for her to disappear for hours at a time in the fields that surrounded her home. It was during one of these times alone, when she was twelve, that she heard the voices of Saints Michael, Catherine, and Margaret.

"She wept from the sheer beauty of it," Infinity said. "And at the sound, she knew instantly who she was and what she was supposed to do in this manifestation—to change life in Europe by driving the English out of France and to publicly announce her reason for doing it was because God spoke to her. In short, her mission was to serve as a living testament to her faith, to show the power of the individual, and to die a martyr."

Joan After the Time of Awareness

From the moment Enumerae, as Joan, recognized her mission on Earth, she was relentless in her journey toward resolution. Within four years of her Time of Awareness, she convinced one of her kinsmen to take her, disguised as a boy, to visit the royal French court where she correctly predicted the success of a planned battle near Orleans. She cited divine inspiration.

Her prediction, and the reasons behind it, made Charles VII, the King of France, aware of her gift. As one of the angels sent to help Enumerae with this manifestation, Charles sent her to Orleans to travel with his army. This recognition, by the man who many believed should rule the whole of France, brought Joan immediately onto the public stage and gave her a voice and a venue to serve as a living testament to her faith.

The crafting of Joan's "story" from that point on was vital to the success of the mission. Everything she said or did was under scrutiny. She had to embody her faith.

It is difficult for us, in today's world where images are manufactured and people are "brands" in and of themselves, to imagine the novelty of how one person can so impact the social and political landscape. But the power of Joan's convictions, combined with her charisma and force of will, was something that few people had ever experienced.

It should also be noted that, to promulgate this message, Joan had to be a religious zealot. Unlike Jesus, who was gentle, kind, and nurturing, Joan was single-minded and more than once argued vehemently with the people who were there to help her, including the angels who had been sent in human form to help exact change.

As had been the case with the angel who was Mary Magdalene with Jesus, and Khadijah with Muhammad, the same energy was sent in human form in this manifestation to be Joan's co-commander, the Duke of Alencon. With his support, she was able to pull off several amazing events that in modern vernacular made her a superstar. Her presence revitalized the war effort and ultimately led to the coronation of Charles VII when the French recaptured the city of Reims. It also made her a target for eventual capture by the English.

According to Infinity, there are striking similarities between the manifestations of Jesus and Joan. Both were positioned to be political pawns, both were religious figureheads, and both were tried and betrayed. For Jesus, betrayal came at the hands of Judas and the leader of the Sanhedrin. For Joan, her betrayer was Charles VII. Though all of these betrayers were angels sent with that specific mission, the parallels and the impact they have had on humanity cannot be ignored.

Just as Jesus was executed for all to see, so, too, was Joan's death a public spectacle that was imbued with spiritual and social significance. Documentation from the time details how she was tied to a tall pillar in the town square. Her lips moved in silent prayer even as faggots of sticks were placed around her feet. Though most did not realize the subtle nod to her earlier manifestation as Jesus, a peasant gave her a small, crude cross.

"She was dignified and stoic even as the torches were held to the wood at her feet," Infinity said. "The poignancy of her execution was elevated by the fact that she prayed until the pain became too much. It was a horrific death. But, by dying as she had lived—an embodiment of her faith—she brought about the change that was desperately needed at the time. Her faith and her death inspired and reinforced the beliefs of Catholics throughout the country and reinvigorated faith in the nation as a whole."

From our standpoint today, it's perhaps easy to think that Joan's message was specific to Catholicism. But that is not the case. Though it was the prevailing belief in Europe (and later spread to the New World), Joan's message was for everyone—a nudge to recognize that to fully live a life of value, one must stand up for what is right and embody the tenets of one's belief. Her legacy endures in that her name is now synonymous with martyrdom, the power of unconditional faith and bravery in the face of seemingly insurmountable odds.

As noted by Infinity, "Joan knew almost from the beginning that she was going to have to become a martyr. She knew that through her faith, she would stand as a beacon—a pillar—and ultimately, a sacrifice. Her actions caused many to reexamine their faith in not just 'God' but also in humanity. It reinvigorated their belief systems and later, their righteousness.

"Joan was a woman who reminded humanity at the time that there was more to life than just poverty and kings and wealth and wars. She was a living illustration that belief in something higher than—something greater than—oneself was necessary if they were to survive and exact change that extended outside of their village or shire."

And that is the lesson we must take from Enumerae's manifestation of Joan. Each of us has the power to make the world a better and more just place. The key is recognizing the power within each of us and then having the bravery to stand up and be heard. What is ironic is that it is both the simplest and yet hardest thing to do.

Book of Martin Luther

When looking at the historical figures into whom Infinity chose to have Enumerae incarnate, we can see clearly that this is not a punitive energy/God/power, but rather, one that is concerned with providing the opportunities necessary for humanity to evolve and mature.

"I am the chaos and the calm," Infinity said. "Though I cannot take away the natural chaos because that is the mechanism for the constant change that is necessary for life on earth to continue, I can provide tools for organizing the chaos. The most basic of these can be found in mathematics and the need for 'balance.'"

Just as there is a balance of Enumerae and Innumerae, so too, exists in the human experience the binary oppositions of everything and nothing—ones and zeros. But there is also, and, according to Infinity, will always will be, the "other"—the middle point upon which these oppositions must balance. This is seen, not only in the trinity of Infinity, Enumerae, and Innumerae, but also in the diversity of the human experience. Take for example the concepts of good and evil; day and night; black and white. They are at odds. But they are also balanced by the existence of behavior that is neither good nor evil, the times of dawn and dusk, and shades of gray.

Key to understanding Infinity's motivations for each of the manifestations detailed in this

Addendum is appreciating the absolute necessity of a counterbalance—one of whom was Martin Luther.

"Joan gave humanity an enduring legacy of unquestioning faith and the power of the individual to exact change," Infinity said. "But over time, humanity became complacent and the Catholic Church began to exert a tremendous amount of power—not just in terms of religious observance, but also in regard to economics and politics. The power of the church grew to the point that Christians no longer had an authentic and individual relationship with God.

"When I sent Enumerae back to earth in the human form of Martin Luther, it was to reaffirm Joan's lesson regarding the power of the individual to bring about change, but also, to provide a counterbalance to those who felt marginalized by the power of the Catholic Church and hungered for a personal relationship with God."

It sounds contrary—to send a manifestation that seems to counteract the work of a previous manifestation. But according to Infinity, it is in accordance with the continuum of change. It is necessary for a continued forward momentum.

"Once a belief system is in the hands of humans, they can—and do—make it whatever they want," Infinity said. "They create whatever they need it to be. And in this instance, what started out as one thing, Jesus's take on how to be a more godly Jew, gave rise to Christianity, which then evolved into Catholicism. But, as Catholicism became more and more hierarchical and widespread, many people felt it evolved into a system that was as much about control of people and material wealth as spirituality."

Luther Before the Time of Awareness

To provide an alternative to the Catholic control of worship and spearhead the belief that everyone, regardless of social status, could have a personal relationship with "God," Enumerae was born into the human form of Martin Luther in 1483.

As had been the case in past manifestations, Martin Luther was an unremarkable child. Like most Europeans at the time, Luther was brought up as a Catholic. And though he was appropriately devout, his interest in religion and the larger spiritual questions didn't come until much later. Groundwork to prepare him for his mission had to occur first.

Unlike Jesus, Muhammad, and Joan, Martin Luther was born into an upper-middle class German family. His father's success as the owner of copper mines and smelters allowed for Luther to receive an extensive formal education. This included religious education.

To this end, Luther was sent to the University of Erfurt when he was nineteen. His father's intent was for him to study the law. What drew his attention, though, was religion and faith, especially as it applied to how humans came to believe. It was likely no surprise to anyone that he chose instead to become a monk.

"It must be remembered that, in human form, Enumerae has all of the attributes and free will of every other person," Infinity said. "It was necessary to hasten Luther's Time of Awareness before he became too mired in the Catholic hierarchy."

According to Infinity, Luther's Time of Awareness came in 1505 when, while returning to the university, lightning struck so close to his horse that he was thrown to the ground and his head struck a rock. It was during this state of unconsciousness that his mission was revealed to him.

Luther After the Time of Awareness

"Once Luther understood what he was charged with accomplishing on earth, he threw himself into the study of theology," Infinity said. "Two of the angels sent to help in this mission were Johann von Staupitz, the dean of the theological faculty at the University of Wittenberg and Philipp Malanchthon. It was under their guidance that Luther began to develop his platform for a radical change in the doctrine of religious observance."

We see this plan being put into action once he was ordained. He very quickly used his position in the church to preach that the Pope and the Roman Catholic Church weren't necessary to have a relationship with "God" and that salvation was a free gift that came through faith, not donating money to the Catholic Church or doing good works.

As we can see, this is a markedly different take on observance and demonstration of belief. To suggest that anyone, regardless of social status, sex, or national origin could have a relationship with Infinity gave all people agency to explore and strengthen their faith.

To further solidify this personal relationship, Luther encouraged the translation of the Bible into German and then utilized the new technology of a printing press to mass produce copies. Suddenly, the "Word of God" was available to anyone who could read. And to further show the distinction between the Catholic Church and what was coming to be called Protestantism, Infinity instructed Luther to strip away the vestiges of separation and make it known that Protestant priests were allowed to marry—which Luther supported in theory and practice when he married Katharina von Bora, a nun he helped escape from a Cistercian convent and who would be his strongest supporter. Katharina was, of course, the angel manifested previously as Mary Magdalene and most recently, as Joan of Arc's co-commander, John II, the Duke of Alencon.

He sent a clear message, not just in his actions, but also in writings such as the *95 Theses,* in which he called for an end to the purchase of indulgences, and in his introduction to the New Testament. His writings were disseminated thanks to the printing press and ultimately exacted social and cultural change.

Clearly, Luther's actions put him in direct opposition to the Catholic Church. Not only was he excommunicated by the Pope, but also tried and convicted as a heretic. Still, in keeping with his mission, Enumerae, as Martin Luther, pressed on. He started his own church in 1522 and encouraged other Protestants to form congregations of their own. He also began to speak out against the Jewish and Islamic belief systems.

"It was his job to be hated by many," Infinity said. "Though he was not assassinated or murdered, as had been the case in previous manifestations, the hatred and persecution Luther endured at the hands of society at large was equally as painful in a different way. For Luther to be successful, he had to be despised. He had to stand as the very public counterbalance to that which already existed."

Martin Luther died at the age of sixty-two. His last sermon was delivered three days before he suffered a stroke and shortly thereafter, died. According to Infinity, Luther's death was necessary to ensure that humanity took up the reigns of the Protestant Reformation and made it their own.

"At some point, humans need to take responsibility for that which I have given them," Infinity said. "Each of the manifestations are catalysts for change. But if what they have created is going to survive, it must be at the hands of the people who needed the new avenue of worship in the first place."

When one thinks about it, this responsibility is in keeping with the reasons for these manifestations in the first place. If we, as humans, truly value that which we are given, we will protect, nurture, and grow the concept. And when it ceases to be relevant?

"It falls by the wayside in favor of something that does work," Infinity said. "No longer do the Greek or Egyptian gods hold a place in modern belief. Rather, they are a fascinating part of human history that are studied and discussed. Their power is diminished."

And perhaps, that is one of the prevailing lessons we should take from this *Addendum*. Though Infinity has the power to provide what we need, it is up to us to nurture and maintain that which we have been given. If we are to take this as true, then it becomes clear that the power—all power—is, and has always been, ours.

Book of Rebecca Nurse

It is interesting to note that in each of Enumerae's manifestations there have been some sort of social, political, or legal judgments leveled. In almost every instance, the human that is Enumerae is forced to stand trial—to be judged both in the legal court and also the court of public approval.

Why is this such a commonality? Is it because we fear that which is new or different and feel the need to tear it down? Is it because we are unsure how to fit that which is unknown into our already established, cozy paradigms? Or, is it that we feel threatened by other people's definition of "right" if it contradicts *our* perceptions of "right"?

According to Infinity, it is all of these. Returning for a moment to the "rules" mentioned in the *Introduction*, just as each of us have our own reality, those realities differ based on the person. And, given the constant of change and the inherent need for balance, these types of "right" or "wrong" categorizations, based on one's personal reality, are normal. Only when there is recognition of the differences can objective discussion occur.

But what does that have to do with the trials (literal and figurative) faced by each of Enumerae's manifestations? It actually sets the stage for examination and discourse.

"Each instance of a trial presented an opportunity to publicly discuss and document the fundamentals of a new belief system," Infinity said. "By raging against these new, and perhaps contradictory concepts, those who sought to oppress it are, in fact, elevating it in importance. This documentation also allowed for retrospection at a later date and, ultimately, an appreciation of a larger, more over-arching life lesson."

Nowhere is this more true than in regard to the Salem Witch Trials of 1692 and 1693, in which an untold number of men, women, and children in Essex, Suffolk, and Middlesex counties in colonial Massachusetts were accused of witchcraft. By the end of the ordeal, more than a hundred-and-fifty people had been arrested and put in prison, with nineteen of those ultimately convicted and executed. Its social significance lives on even today in the vernacular of persecution in the form of a "witch hunt."

"Though it was a trial conducted in the name of religion, the Salem Witch Trials were as much designed to be a lesson on persecution and intolerance as anything else," Infinity said. "The decision to send Enumerae in the human form of Rebecca Nurse, an elderly, devout Puritan, was designed to be shocking."

And, it *is* shocking to think of a seventy-two-year-old woman being executed as a result of fear and religious oppression. But, according to Infinity, it was necessary to show what can happen when religion and religious leaders assume legal responsibility for civil matters.

Rebecca Before the Time of Awareness

"When Enumerae was sent to earth in the form of Rebecca Towne, later to become Rebecca Nurse, it was with the mission of drawing attention to the need for separation between religious and civil oversight," Infinity said. "The people of colonial Massachusetts were some of the first to take their religion and move to a new continent where they were left to govern themselves. This isolation allowed for either the best or the worst aspects of human behavior to emerge. In anticipation of the latter, I believed it was necessary to put a mechanism in place to illustrate how religion can be used as a weapon if it evolves into mob mentality."

According to Infinity, Rebecca was born in 1621 in England. She moved with her family to Salem Village as part of a wave of colonists in 1640, and married her husband, Francis Nurse, in 1644. As had been the case in previous manifestations, Enumerae, as Rebecca, was rather ordinary. As did most women of her day, she worked on the family homestead and took care of her husband and children. Throughout her life she was a devout Puritan and a model citizen—at first because it was expected of her and later, because she had to live an untarnished life if she were to be martyred.

Enumerae, in the human form of Rebecca, was made aware of her mission on her birthday, February 21, in 1690—a little more than two years before her death. At the age of seventy, she was an invalid who did little more than go to church and spend time with her family. Given her age and frailty, a traumatic event to trigger her awareness was not possible.

"She was napping by the fire in the early afternoon when I sent her a vision in the form of a dream," Infinity said. "In the dream, I made her aware of her true self and the mission with which she had been charged—that despite her piety and righteous life, she was going to be tried, condemned, and executed for crimes she did not commit so that she could stand as an example for the need of separation of government and religion, and as an illustration for the result of mob mentality in the name of religion."

As part of this dream, Infinity revealed that angels, manifested in human form, would play specific roles in the ordeal. The most notable of these were: Judge John Hawthorne, one of her accusers, Ann Putnam, Jr., and Rebecca's sister, Sarah Cloyce, who also was accused, but survived. The angel manifested previously as Mary Magdalene was her close friend who was never identified in court records or historical documents. According to Infinity, each had a role to play in ensuring that, despite the public outrage at Rebecca's trial, she be executed.

Rebecca After the Time of Awareness

To understand why the Salem Witch Trials occurred, we must return to the idea that the rules for religious doctrine and observance are human constructs. *How* a group prays to or honors their god or belief system is not determined by Infinity. For the Puritans, these rules were based on the existence of two worlds—the visible world and one that couldn't be seen, but that was inhabited by God and his angels, who were in constant battle with Satan and his demons. Within Puritan society, women were considered the weaker sex and, as such, were especially prey to the Devil and his demons—which was why, when Betty Parris and her cousin Abigail Williams began to have fits, Betty's father, Rev. Samuel Parris, believed it was the work of the devil.

At first, the accusations focused on three women—all of whom were considered outcasts or misfits. A month later, five more women were arrested, including Rebecca Nurse and Martha Corey—both of whom were full, covenanted members of their churches. What came next was the creation of a climate of distrust, incrimination, and mass hysteria. Men and women were being arrested, interrogated, and either charged, or, if they admitted guilt and incriminated others, released.

"The situation spiraled quickly out of control," Infinity said. "The only way to make the people of the region aware of just how badly, was to allow them to do something shocking—to execute a person who was clearly innocent. That person, of course, was Rebecca Nurse."

According to Infinity, Enumerae, in the human form of Rebecca, was allowed to become elderly and physically frail before being made aware of her mission. That she was clearly innocent and physically compromised, but still tried and executed, was necessary for her to stand as testament to the injustice and murder being committed in the name of religious righteousness. It was also important that the proceedings be documented as a testament to the travesty of justice that occurred.

It is telling that Rebecca Nurse was tried more than once for the same crime. When she was found "not guilty" at the first trial, the jury was instructed to reconsider the verdict. After a significant amount of pressure from the leaders of the religious community, they changed the verdict to "guilty." The governor at the time pardoned her on the basis of what he saw as manufactured charges, though that decision was later reversed.

Rebecca was sentenced to death on June 30, 1692, excommunicated July 3, 1692, and executed sixteen days later. But that wasn't the end. All told, over the course of the year-and-a-half-long situation, an untold number of men and women were tried.

"The lesson for all of this came much later," Infinity said. "Though the injustice was evident at the time—and noted by many—only later did the much larger implications of this social, cultural, and religious travesty become clear."

It's said that hindsight is twenty-twenty—that only in retrospect can we see things clearly. If that is indeed the case, what then does hindsight reveal to us as we consider the trial of Rebecca Nurse? What lessons can we take, not just from her experience, but also from the lives of Jesus, Muhammad, Joan, and Martin Luther?

Book of Joseph Smith

As has been noted in *Continuations,* each of Infinity's manifestations of Enumerae in human form have been designed to encourage faith, illustrate the power of the individual to exact change, and encourage humanity to be more compassionate and tolerant. Sometimes that worked. Other times it didn't.

These are not easy lessons to learn—or at least to put into practice. Forgiveness. Compassion. Tolerance. Infinity has sent Enumerae to the earth multiple times to help us learn these principles. Some of Enumerae's manifestations have been religious figures. Some have been political figures. Some have been a mixture of the two. Regardless of how the message is delivered, though, the meaning is about having tolerance for that which is different.

As mentioned previously, no religious belief system can be proven as fact, just as none can be disproven as false. The power, for all belief, is faith—even if the core of a belief system may seem nonsensical to others. And nowhere is this more evident than in the creation of a system of belief known as the Latter-day Saints movement.

Joseph Before the Time of Awareness

Enumerae, in the human form of Joseph Smith, Jr., was born December 23, 1805, in Vermont.

Unlike in previous manifestations, Joseph was a remarkable child in regard to his maturity and faith in God.

According to Infinity, this was intentional because, like Jesus and Joan, he would be assassinated while still fairly young, which meant that there was a great deal he had to accomplish. For that reason, when he was seven years old, Joseph contracted typhoid. Though he seemed to recover, the affliction later reappeared as a bone infection in his leg. To avoid amputation, it was decided that doctors would peel away the skin and chip out the diseased bone. Because of his religious beliefs, Joseph refused alcohol, which was the "modern" method of surgical pain relief for the time.

"The pain was excruciating, but it was necessary to jar Joseph into recognition of his true nature and the mission with which he had been charged," Infinity said. "It was also a precursor for the trials to come."

According to Infinity, Joseph's family endured a variety of hardships—both financial and personal. During much of Joseph's childhood the family bounced from state to state based on Joseph Sr.'s ability to find work. Eventually, after losing their crop to a summer frost, they followed Joseph Sr.'s brother to western New York state where Joseph Jr. was exposed to the teachings of the Protestant revivalism movement. He was twelve.

"It was important for him to have a solid understanding of this new perception of religious reality in the United States," Infinity said. "This attention to addressing society's ills, before what many of the practitioners believed was the imminent second coming of Jesus, was key to his role for what was to come."

Joseph After the Time of Awareness

According to Infinity, though Joseph knew of his mission and had been preparing himself for years, it wasn't until he was fourteen that he was able to actively begin to implement the plan. As has been the case with previous manifestations, Joseph spent a great deal of his time alone, walking through the woods on the family's land.

"Much of our discussion about the implementation of this new religious belief system occurred during these periods of solitude," Infinity said. "As we waited and judged the religious and political climate of the revivalist movement, it became clear that for this system to work, it needed to incorporate familiar tenets while presenting a fresh means of worship.

"As had been the case with Innumerae, in the human form of Moses, and his receipt of two stone tablets containing the Ten Commandments, it was determined that Joseph would receive his message on golden plates. These plates, which weighed about fifty pounds, were engraved with Egyptian-looking hieroglyphs on both sides and bound with three D-shaped rings. The information on the plates, in addition to visions and visitations by angels, would constitute the message to be contained in the new religious text, which would be presented in a way that was similar to the Christian Bible."

And indeed, when one looks at the resulting

Book of Mormon, there are several similarities to the King James Version of the Christian Bible—most notably that it is divided into fifteen "books" that document previously unknown events in history as detailed by a series of narrators.

The narrative, as translated and transcribed by Joseph Smith in the Book of Mormon, is the story of a divinely-favored group of Israelites who are led from Jerusalem to the North American continent in the 580s BCE, shortly after the fall of Babylon. Once in what is now the United States, the founding family, headed by the prophet Lehi, settled. As is seen in Genesis, jealousy and discord between his sons, Nephi and Laman evolves into a feud. Over time the sons separate into warring factions that eventually became two different civilizations.

The first narrators include Nephi and his descendants. The majority of the story, however, is inscribed on the golden plates by a Nephite soldier named Mormon. Toward the end of his life, Mormon turned the task of documentation to his son, Moroni, who compiled additional information on the people of the region and added letters that had been written by his father. Once completed, Moroni buried the plates on the hill where Joseph was later sent to find them. By 400 CE, the people detailed in the Book of Mormon had been replaced by their descendants, the people we today call Native Americans.

"It's a fantastical story to be sure," Infinity said. "But, like any story upon which religion is based, it is one that must be taken as a matter of faith. In all instances of religious belief systems, it is what it provides for those who believe that is important, not whether it can be proven or if it makes sense."

And, if we think about this objectively, it's true. Consider for a moment the stories that form the basis of any belief system and it is clear that one commonality is that they often strain the bounds of credulity. Whether it is belief in an omnipotent human-esque figure in the heavens, the idea that humans in the form of *thetans* are the product of extraterrestrial cultures that came to live on this planet, or that the human soul is continually reborn into a new body after biological death, adherence to *all* belief systems is based on faith. To accept that any belief system, when objectively deconstructed actually makes little sense, we can immediately level the playing field and focus on the role that faith plays in peoples' lives. And given that Mormonism is currently the fastest growing religion in the world, it's clear that its message resonates with many.

Given that growth, it's important to look at how the message of Mormonism came be disseminated and find its audience. According to Infinity, Enumerae, as Joseph, worked with angels manifested into human form, to write an account of what was engraved on the golden plates. One of the most important of these was Joseph's human wife, Emma, who had previously manifested as Mary Magdalene, Khadijah, and the Duke of Alencon. Also re-manifested was Oliver Cowdery, who helped with the transcription and Edbert B. Grandin, who, in 1830, published and sold the first copies, and Joseph's brother Hyrum, who was integral in helping establish the church.

"Society had evolved in such a way that dissemination was both easier and more complicated," Infinity said. "Many more copies could be produced in a shorter period of time, but with so much available to read, people had to be enticed by the content, which is why, the same year the Book of Mormon was published, I instructed Enumerae to organize a church that was a restoration of the early Christian church. Those for whom this new take on religion resonated would be called Latter-day Saints."

As membership in the Mormon church grew, Joseph was instructed by Infinity to build "American Zions" in Kirtland, Ohio and Independence, Missouri. He was also instructed to send out missionaries and print new revelations—all of which were designed to appeal to the faithful and anger the non-Mormons.

In both instances, non-members of the church railed against those who believed. Entire villages were burned and the faithful were forced to flee their homes. After the Missouri governor signed the Mormon Execution Order into law, Smith moved his followers to Illinois where they turned a swampy, mosquito-infested patch of land into a prosperous new city called Nauvoo. As mayor, Smith became the spiritual and political leader.

"As had been the case in previous manifestations, Enumerae in the human form of Joseph, ultimately had to be martyred in the name of his teachings," Infinity said. "For Joseph, this came in 1844 at the hands of non-Mormons critical of the tenets of his belief system."

Joseph Smith's end came when an angry mob

of non-Mormons stormed the jail in Carthage, Missouri, where Joseph and his brother, Hyrum, were being held. They had been jailed for allegedly destroying the printing press of a paper that was critical of Mormon doctrine and which had accused Joseph of practicing polygamy. Though five members of the mob were tried, none were found guilty.

According to Infinity, by the time Joseph was murdered, there were tens of thousands of practitioners of the Mormon faith—enough for it to live or die on its own merits. And, as we know, Mormonism not only survived, but eventually thrived under the leadership of Brigham Young, who ultimately led the followers to Utah.

There continues to be a great deal of mistrust and skepticism about Mormonism. Those outside the faith argue that it's nonsensical and is contradicted by genetics and the archaeological record. But, in the end, does it really matter? If the faith started by Joseph Smith and carried forward by his successors resonates with a segment of the human population and provides them with a code of behavior that makes them more moral in their actions, whose place is it to judge? And more to the point, why should we want to?

Book of Mohandas Gandhi

Infinity has been clear from the onset that the points of each of the manifestations of Innumerae and Enumerae into human form have been engineered as catalysts for change and to provide an opportunity for awareness of larger life lessons. In previous manifestations we have seen Enumerae teach kindness, forgiveness, tolerance, and standing up for one's beliefs in the face of consternation and condemnation. In this, the most recent manifestation, we see all of these attributes embodied in one man—Mohandas Karamchand Gandhi.

It could be argued that Enumerae, manifested as the human form of Gandhi, was born into a world that was more interdependent, complex, and divisive than at any time in the past. Nowhere was this more evident than in India where, over the course of Gandhi's life, Hindu extremists were so set against the Muslims and Christians of the region that they demanded their own nation state. This political strife, combined with segregation based not only on religion, but also ethnicity and caste, created an atmosphere that was a powder keg waiting to explode.

"What was occurring in India was a harbinger for what was to come for the rest of the world if humankind couldn't learn tolerance and acceptance of diversity," Infinity said. "Too many people inhabited the world for such issues to divide them, which is why I sent Enumerae in the form of a quiet, unassuming man who would stand as a global testament to the power of non-violent protest, civil rights, and forgiveness."

Gandhi Before the Time of Awareness

According to Infinity, Enumerae's mission in the human form of Gandhi was different and more complicated than any of the previous manifestations.

"The change that Gandhi was tasked with bringing about was, for the first time ever, not specific to practitioners of a particular belief in a region, country, or continent," Infinity said. "What Gandhi was asked to accomplish was to bring to the world's attention the endemic problems of racism, prejudice, and the atrocities that can occur in any religion if left unchecked."

Gandhi was born in the coastal town of Porbandar in western India on October 2, 1869, to parents in the Vaishya caste of the Hindu Caste System. His father was the chief minister of the Porbandar state, which gave Gandhi certain advantages. According to Infinity, it was important that he be born into a higher caste so he could, like Martin Luther before him, be educated and properly prepared to complete his mission.

"Gandhi was, like the other manifestations, a decidedly average child," Infinity said. "He was not a good student, was not particularly devout, and spent most of his time alone reading books. The one distinguishing characteristic he possessed, and which would become more pronounced over time, was an emotional maturity and awareness of the values of truth and love for others."

At the age of thirteen, in keeping with tradition at the time, Gandhi was married to Kasturbaj Makhanji. As had been the case in the past, she was an angel that previously had been Mary Magdalene, Joan of Arc's co-commander, John II, Duke of Alencon, and Joseph Smith's wife, Emma. According to Infinity, theirs was a happy marriage that produced four children.

In 1888, Gandhi's father sent him to London, England to study law. While there, though he was exposed to Western society, he continued to abstain from alcohol and practice vegetarianism. It was this latter observance and his membership in the Vegetarian Society that led to interaction with scholars of Buddhist and Hindu literature. Their suggestion that he read the *Bhagavad Gita,* a sacred Hindu text that ties together the concepts of morality, liberation, and selfless action, was an integral part of Gandhi's preparation for his mission.

After law school, Gandhi returned to India where he worked for two years before accepting a position in South Africa working for the Muslim Indian Traders. While there, he experienced many times the discrimination common for all people with dark skin. However, it was only when he was travelling by stagecoach and was beaten for refusing to give up his seat to a European passenger, that he experienced his Time of Awareness.

"The beating, done out of such prejudice and injustice, was a necessary impetus to Gandhi's message," Infinity said. "That act, which was perpetrated by a normal human, illustrated the inequities seen throughout the world based on skin color."

Again, hindsight allows us to see the big picture, but if we stop for a moment and consider human nature and our need to categorize and compartmentalize everything from our silverware to humans based on non-existent classifications of race, it becomes clear that defining "the other" (which can often be read as "less than") is inherent in who we are. And, the less that people have in common with a particular group, the easier it is to justify discriminating against and subjugating them.

It's easy to look back in time and point to examples of this. The Assyrians, the Greeks and Romans, the Europeans in the Americas . . . all of these are examples of societies who subjugated, enslaved, and, in some instances, tried to exterminate others. To bring it into specific relief, consider for a moment what was going on throughout the world during the first part of Gandhi's lifetime. Though slavery had been abolished in the United States, discrimination and violence against people with dark skin (African and Native Americans) was prevalent. In the "Old World," thousands of years of discrimination against the Jews (from seemingly every corner) was beginning to coalesce into what would eventually manifest as the Holocaust.

Gandhi After the Time of Awareness

As Enumerae, in the human form of Gandhi, realized what was expected in this manifestation, the skills that had been learned before the Time of

Awareness became invaluable. Gandhi began to actively advocate on the part of Indians in South Africa—first in opposing a bill denying Indians the right to vote and then in 1894, forming a Natal Indian Congress that unified the Indian community.

"It was important that Gandhi's actions be very public, very political, and very evocative," Infinity said. "His message had to evoke passion—both on the part of the people being protected and those who were opposed. We knew his message had struck a chord when, in 1897, he was attacked by a mob of angry white settlers when he arrived in Durban. By his refusal to press charges, it also allowed us to begin what would become his signature message of nonviolence and forgiveness."

According to Infinity, this was also an opportunity for Gandhi to begin laying the groundwork for peaceful resistance as a mechanism to bring about social change—a plan he put into practice while in South Africa as he spearheaded a nonviolent protest campaign for rights for all Indians in the country.

Though not entirely successful in securing rights for his people, the notoriety Gandhi gained—both because of his methods of passive resistance and the international attention his many arrests in the name of Indian rights garnered—afforded him a platform for his true mission when Infinity sent him back to India in 1915.

"To be the catalyst for such a significant cultural change in thought, Gandhi had to become a living manifestation of his philosophy and then be martyred for it," Infinity said. "As a member, and later, leader of the Indian National Congress, it was essential that he advocate for the rights of all. At first, he focused on peasants' rights and later, Muslim political inclusion—this despite the historic animosity that existed between the Hindus and Muslims."

This multi-cultural base of support was necessary for Infinity's next task—to lead the fight for India's independence from the British Empire by launching a non-violent non-cooperation campaign. Millions of Indians supported the cause despite the incidences of violence, imprisonment, and sometimes death of the participants.

Although the campaign was eventually successful, becoming an independent state opened the door for renewed hostilities between the Hindu and Muslims—namely, an escalation of the increasing violence between the different religious groups. As a means of ending the violence, a portion of India was partitioned in 1947 and a new Muslim country was created—Pakistan.

"As I have noted before, humans have free will," Infinity said. "The decision to create this new country and the continued violence made it clear that it was time for Gandhi to engage in his final hunger strike in non-violent protest and prepare for his assassination."

Gandhi was seventy-eight years old on January 20, 1948, when he was shot three times in the chest while on his way to speak at a prayer meeting. His assassin—the same angel who had manifested in the human forms of Caiaphas, the president of the Sanhedrin, and Charles VII—was Nathuram Godse, a Hindu extremist who accused Gandhi of favoring Pakistan.

"Gandhi's death evoked worldwide mourning," Infinity said. "People of all faiths attended local ceremonies honoring his contributions to society, his messages of compassion, equality, and forgiveness, and his embodiment of those ideals."

Even to this day, mention of the name Gandhi evokes images of a small, bespectacled man with a gentle smile—a man who was the embodiment of humanitarianism. His message lives on in the global social construct and even inspired the methods of other civil rights activists—most famously, Nelson Mandela and Martin Luther King, Jr., who, too, was assassinated.

But was Gandhi's message enough? Did it change anything in the long term? Every day we see examples of genocide, racism, and subjugation of those deemed "lesser." Even today there is continued strife between Hindu and Muslim groups. If there was to be change, shouldn't we see it by now?

According to Infinity, we have.

"Change is the one constant," Infinity said. "Sometimes that change is immediate like a thunderbolt. And other times, it's slow and must seep into the social consciousness. As humans tire of the divisions between themselves and realize that the world is too interconnected to continue on in such a divisive manner, my hope is that they will change. Rather than using bullets and bombs, I envision a future in which Gandhi's message will be taken to heart and people instead will use words and ideas."

CONCLUSIONS

"Though Gandhi was the most recent manifestation of Enumerae in human form, I can assure humanity that it will not be the last," Infinity said. "My love for your welfare is infinite and I will continue to provide opportunities for change and unification. The stories contained in this *Addendum* are proof of that."

And indeed, that is the case. In each manifestation, humanity was provided with an opportunity to consider something greater than themselves—a concept, a belief system, or a life lesson.

Though their objectives and roles in history differed, Infinity repeatedly provided us with the opportunity to take to heart certain moral imperatives—concepts and life lessons that are universal. The commonalities of kindness, forgiveness, and tolerance are not the property of just one "right" religious belief system. *They are seen in all religions.* Regardless of whether we call it the Golden Rule or the Law of One, the message is the same:

- Christianity: "All things whatsoever ye would that men should do to you, do ye so to them; for this is the law and the prophets." Matthew 7:1
- Judaism: "What is hateful to you, do not do to your fellow men. This is the entire Law: all the rest is commentary." Talmud, Shabbat 3id

- Islam: "No one of you is a believer until he desires for his brother that which he desires for himself." Sunnah
- Buddhism: "Hurt not others in ways that you yourself would find hurtful." Udana-Varga 5:1
- Hinduism: "This is the sum of Dharma; do naught onto others what you would not have them do unto you." Mahabharata 5:1517
- Confucianism: "Do not do to others what you would not like yourself." Analects 12:22
- Sikhism: "Don't create enmity with anyone as God is within everyone." Guru Arjan Devji 259
- Native American Spirituality: "Respect for all life is the foundation." The Great Law of Peace
- Baha'i: "Ascribe not to any soul that which thou wouldst not have ascribed to thee, and say not that which thou doest not." Baha'u'llah
- Humanism: "Humanists affirm that individual and social problems can only be resolved by means of human reason, intelligent effort, critical thinking joined with compassion, and a spirit of empathy for all living things." British Humanist Society (11)
- Paganism (Roman): "The law imprinted on the hearts of all men is to love the members of society as themselves."
- Wicca: "And it harm none, do what thou wilt." Wiccan Rede
- Ancient Egyptian translation: "Do for one who may do for you, that you may cause him thus to do." The Tale of the Eloquent Peasant 109-110
- Jainism: "A man should wander about treating all creatures as he himself would be treated." Sutrakritanga 1.11.33

The Dalai Lama said, "Every religion emphasizes human improvement, love, respect for others, sharing other people's suffering. On these lines every religion had more or less the same viewpoint and the same goal."

If this is true and we all share essentially the same ultimate credo, why then is religious belief so divisive? Why, if we have had the opportunity time after time to be kind, to forgive, and be tolerant, do we use our free will to engage in warfare, subjugation, slavery, violence, hatred, and persecution? Why do we let the differences separate us instead of the similarities unite us? Maybe it's because we, as humans, have never had a common enemy. We have only had ourselves to battle so we seek out those tiny differences in each other.

Infinity acknowledged being everything and nothing—not just here for us, but everywhere in the universe. If that is indeed the case, what if there exist other life forms, other energies, other . . . beings? Would knowledge of them and their differences from us unify us as a species? Would we see each other as brothers and sisters in alliance against this new "other"?

Perhaps. Perhaps not. It's just one more thing that we don't yet know.

Humans are a young species. Whether you believe we were created by the hand of a god a little more than six thousand years ago or evolved from a common ancestor hundreds of thousands of years ago, the fact remains that we are young. We are still learning and still figuring out our place in the world. And as we go about this journey, it's vital that if nothing else, we remember that we are—every one of us—a part of the collective whole. We are a globalized village that is interconnected and interdependent in ways not even fathomable in the past.

It is Infinity's desire that humanity celebrates and accepts our differences, even as we embrace that which is common to all. That is the reason for this *Addendum,* and the message it contains.

"Each of you—no matter the color of your skin, your social status, or the power you choose (or not) to worship—is part of a cohesive whole," Infinity said. "Regardless of surface differences, you are all, in my eyes, equal and precious. My hope is that someday, you will understand that I see and value each of you for your differences as much as for your similarities."

This is a lesson that every single one of us needs to take to heart. The planet we inhabit, the resources that we utilize, the decisions we make individually, impact the whole. There is no better or worse, just different. And it is only when we ask questions that challenge what we think we know, that we grow and gain true understanding.

We are, all of us, "equal and precious" in Infinity's eyes. If Infinity doesn't distinguish, why should we? Given that we're all the same, isn't it time we started acting like it?

ABOUT THE AUTHOR

Before being commissioned by Infinity to write and market *The Addendum* for Infinity Press, Sarah Sheppard was an advertising executive for Marshall & Associates in New York, NY.

Before working for M&A, Sarah worked as an account executive for Nuance Marketing in New York City, and as an account representative for K. Henderson & Associates in Chicago. She is a native of Nebraska and received her degree in marketing and mass communications from the University of Nebraska in Lincoln.

She considers herself a supporter of all religious belief systems.

www.ingramcontent.com/pod-product-compliance
Ingram Content Group UK Ltd.
Pitfield, Milton Keynes, MK11 3LW, UK
UKHW020223250726
13967UKWH00001B/156

9 781939 562623